DISCARDED

HANNAH *and* SUGAR

WORDS AND PICTURES BY

KATE BERUBE

ABRAMS BOOKS FOR YOUNG READERS
NEW YORK

THE ILLUSTRATIONS IN THIS BOOK WERE CREATED WITH INK, FLASHE PAINT, AND ACRYLIC PAINT ON COLD PRESS WATERCOLOR PAPER.

Library of Congress Cataloging-in-Publication Data

Berube, Kate, author, illustrator.
Hannah and Sugar / by Kate Berube.
pages cm
Summary: "Every day after school, Hannah sees her classmate's dog, Sugar. Hannah politely declines to pet Sugar, because Hannah is afraid of dogs. But one day, Sugar goes missing, and it's Hannah who finds him"— Provided by publisher.
ISBN 978-1-4197-1890-8
[1. Dogs—Fiction. 2. Fear—Fiction.] I. Title.
PZ7.1.B465Han 2016
[E]—dc23
2015017235

Text and illustrations copyright © 2016 Kate Berube
Book design by Chad W. Beckerman

Published in 2016 by Abrams Books for Young Readers, an imprint of ABRAMS. All rights reserved. No portion of this book may be reproduced, stored in a retrieval system, or transmitted in any form or by any means, mechanical, electronic, photocopying, recording, or otherwise, without written permission from the publisher.

Printed and bound in China
10 9 8 7 6 5 4 3 2 1

Abrams Books for Young Readers are available at special discounts when purchased in quantity for premiums and promotions as well as fundraising or educational use. Special editions can also be created to specification. For details, contact specialsales@abramsbooks.com or the address below.

ABRAMS
THE ART OF BOOKS SINCE 1949
115 West 18th Street
New York, NY 10011
www.abramsbooks.com

For Mark

Every day after school, Hannah's papa picked her up at the bus stop.

And every day after school, Sugar was at the bus stop waiting for Violet P.

Every day after school,
Mrs. P. asked Hannah if
she wanted to pet Sugar.

And every day after
school, Hannah said,
"No, thank you."

Every day after school, Hannah's papa picked her up at the bus stop,

and every day, Sugar was at the bus stop waiting for Violet P.

Every day after school, Mrs. P. asked Hannah if she wanted to pet Sugar,

and every single day, Hannah said, “No, thank you.”

But one day, something was different.
“Sugar is missing!” said Violet P.

“She’s been gone all night and all day. No one can find her.”
Everyone promised to help look for Sugar.

Everyone searched high and low . . .

And here and there . . .

But soon it was time to go home for dinner.

. . . and low and high.

. . . and everywhere else, too.

And there was still no sign of Sugar.

After dinner Hannah watched the stars come out.
She listened to the sound of the trains in the distance
and she wondered how it would feel to be lost in the dark.

She decided that it would be scary and that if she were lost
she would be sad and probably hungry.

Then she heard a strange sound. A little whimper.

It was coming from the side of the house. She heard it again.

She tried to see what was making the sound. But it was too dark.

She crawled in between two bushes and saw . . .

Sugar!

Hannah gasped.
She started to back out.
But then she stopped.

Hannah closed her eyes and took a deep breath.

Then she gently reached out her trembling hand.

Sugar sniffed Hannah's hand and rubbed her face along it.

Hannah's papa was very proud of her!

And Violet P. and Mr. and Mrs. P. were so happy to see Sugar.

After that, every day after school,
Hannah's papa picked her up at the
bus stop.

And every day after school,
Sugar was at the bus stop
waiting for Violet P.

31333045229448

And for Hannah, too.